GAME DAY
BASKETBALL
AN INTERACTIVE SPORTS STORY

BY BRANDON TERRELL
ILLUSTRATED BY FRAN BUENO

CAPSTONE PRESS
a capstone imprint

You Choose Books are published by Capstone Press, an imprint of Capstone.
1710 Roe Crest Drive
North Mankato, Minnesota 56003
www.capstonepub.com

Library of Congress Cataloging-in-Publication Data
Names: Terrell, Brandon, 1978- author. | Bueno, Fran, illustrator.
Title: Game day basketball : an interactive sports story / by Brandon
Terrell ; [illustrated by Fran Bueno].
Description: North Mankato, Minnesota : Capstone Press, [2021] | Series:
You choose: Game day sports | Audience: Ages 8-11. | Audience: Grades
4-6. | Summary: It is the basketball championship game and the reader's
choices can mean the difference between a triumphant victory and a
heartbreaking loss.
Identifiers: LCCN 2020039273 (print) | LCCN 2020039274 (ebook) | ISBN
9781496696021 (hardcover) | ISBN 9781496697110 (paperback) | ISBN
9781977154262 (ebook pdf)
Subjects: LCSH: Plot-your-own stories. | CYAC: Basketball--Fiction. |
Plot-your-own stories.
Classification: LCC PZ7.T273 Gam 2021 (print) | LCC PZ7.T273 (ebook) |
DDC [Fic]--dc23
LC record available at https://lccn.loc.gov/2020039273
LC ebook record available at https://lccn.loc.gov/2020039274

Editorial Credits
Editor: Angie Kaelberer; Designer: Kayla Rossow; Media Researcher: Eric Gohl;
Premedia Specialist: Katy LaVigne

TABLE OF CONTENTS

ABOUT YOUR GAME

YOU are a talented basketball player who has used your skills to help your team reach the championship game. But there's just one problem. Your school has never won the championship, while your opponent has won the title many times in the past. People say your team is cursed when playing this team. Can you put your superstitions aside to help lead your team to victory?

Chapter 1 sets the scene. Then you choose which path to read. Follow the directions at the bottom of the page as you read. The decisions you make will change your outcome. After you finish one path, go back and read the others for new perspectives and more adventures.

CHAPTER 1

THE EDGEVIEW CURSE

"Argh! Where are they?"

Your room is a mess. Books, sports equipment, and clothes are scattered around the floor. You lift a pair of sweatpants to look underneath them. No luck.

Your dad appears in your doorway. "Are you ready to go?" he asks.

You shake your head. "I need my lucky socks," you tell him.

"Those stinky old things?" he asks. "They're in the laundry room."

Turn the page.

You dash down the stairs. Your older brother, Nick, is at the bottom, and you nearly crash into him. "Whoa!" he says, spinning in a circle. "Save that speed for the court, bro!"

You ignore him, hurrying into the laundry room. Stacks of clean clothes sit on a table. Are your lucky socks among them? You hope not. You're crazy superstitious, and you haven't washed them since your basketball team went on a winning streak. Today is the championship game, and if the luck has been washed from your socks, you don't know what will happen.

You spy a hint of white with two green stripes poking out from the dirty clothes on the floor.

You sigh with relief, pluck the dirty socks from the pile, and slip them on your bare feet. You wiggle your toes. "Perfect."

Your family piles into the car. You sit with Nick in the back seat.

"So," he says, "are you nervous about the Edgeview Curse?"

You stare at Nick. How could he bring up the curse now?

The Edgeview Middle School Tigers have never won a championship before. They've made it to the big game—Nick was on the team two of those times—but they've never won.

"We're on a hot streak," you tell him. "I think we've got a great chance."

Nick sighs and looks out his window. "Yeah," he says. "I remember thinking that too."

At school, you walk past the trophy case on your way to the locker room. It's filled with second-place and participation trophies. They're constant reminders of the school's history.

To make matters worse, today you'll face the same team Nick lost to when he played. The same team that's won the championship too many times to count—the Haverford Vipers.

Most of your teammates are already in the locker room. Speedy Saddiq Omar. Liu Zhang, the team's assist leader. The tall Duncan "Dunc" Greene. And Charlie Peretti, the most superstitious of all. Just like you, he's wearing a lucky pair of dirty socks. He's doing the same routine he's done before every game—chewing gum with his earbuds in, listening to music. Coach Willis is there too.

"OK, team," he says. Charlie pops out his earbuds. You lace up your sneakers. "Here's the starting lineup."

To play point guard and lead the team, turn to page 13.

To show off your jump shot at small forward, turn to page 51.

To take it to the paint and play center, turn to page 79.

CHAPTER 2

MAKING THE PLAYS

The Tigers are on a roll, and part of the reason is that you've taken charge, leading the way as the team's starting point guard. And you're ready to do it again.

Coach Willis leads the way onto the court. The crowd in the gymnasium is electric. You've experienced big crowds this season. But tonight is more than you expected.

You jog onto the court and take your position. At center, Dunc prepares for the tip-off. You see the Viper point guard, Miles Ortega. He's one of the best players in the state.

The ref blows the whistle, and Dunc leaps up for the tip-off. The Viper center flips it back to Miles, who hurries the ball up the court.

Turn the page.

It's clear the Vipers are playing with an intensity you haven't experienced before. They're fast. Miles passes the ball off to another Viper, who easily drains a jump shot.

The quick, easy score makes you feel uncomfortable. This style of play isn't what led you to the championship. From the sidelines, Coach Willis shouts, "Settle down! Get into a rhythm!"

You get the ball and dribble up the court. The game hinges on how you want to play it. It's time to decide.

To slow down the game, go to page 15.
To keep pace with the Vipers, turn to page 26.

Coach Willis is right. The Tigers made it here playing in their own style. There's no way you're going to change that now.

You take a deep breath, steady yourself, and bring the ball up the court. When you reach the top of the key, you see Miles crouching low, watching you intently. You shout out your favorite play, "Tiger Roar," and your team moves with skill. As they spread out, you spy Liu open on your left. You quickly feed him the ball. He dishes it to Dunc in the lane. Dunc turns and makes an easy layup.

"Yes!" you shout, pumping your fist.

Your slow play doesn't change the way the Vipers are playing. Miles rushes the ball up the court and feeds the ball to his small forward, Brent Reilly.

Turn the page.

Brent sweeps past Charlie, who was barely able to make it back on defense. Brent makes an easy layup, giving the Vipers the lead again.

The game continues this way. Each time you try to slow down the game, the Vipers speed it back up. They're relentless. And playing to their level is wearing down your team.

As you bring the ball up the court again, you have another chance to slow things down. You'll call an easy play, something that you've run a million times before.

To run a motion offense, go to page 17.
To run a give-and-go offense, turn to page 20.

You hold up your right hand in a peace sign, the signal for motion offense. By running it, you're showing the team they need to treat this game just like any other.

Liu sweeps beneath the hoop, moving from right to left. As he does, Dunc plants himself in front of Liu's defender. You bounce the ball to an open Liu in the corner. He puts up a three-pointer and drains it!

The Tigers go on a run, scoring each time down the court and denying the Vipers.

Near the end of the first half, you're ahead by double digits. You dribble down the court. Miles drapes himself all over you, making it hard to drive or pass the ball. But you have to do something.

To pass the ball to a teammate, turn to page 18.
To keep the ball and take the shot, turn to page 19.

If you can dribble past Miles, you'll have a clear lane to the hoop. But then you see two Viper defenders close the gap and realize your chances of making a shot are slim.

Charlie is open, so you dish the ball off to him. But Miles swats it away, and another Viper scoops it up.

"Time-out!" Miles makes a T with his hands, and the ref blows the whistle.

Time is running out in the first half. And after the time-out, Miles leads the Vipers on a roaring comeback. By the time the buzzer sounds, your lead is slim.

Turn to page 38.

You know you can get past Miles. And with a quick step-slide to your left, you breeze by him. But as you do, two Viper defenders close the hole you're driving down. They plant their feet, standing straight up and raising their arms high.

As you go in for the left-handed layup, your hip connects with a Viper defender. He falls to the floor.

Tweep!

The ref stops play. "Foul, offense!" he shouts, pointing at you. "Charging!"

He jogs to the sideline, where the Vipers are set to inbound the ball.

Turn to page 22.

Motion offense is a basic, standard play. Miles and the Vipers may be expecting that. Instead, you quickly perform a crossover dribble and dish the ball to Dunc, who's raced up to the free-throw line.

Miles turns to double-team Dunc, and you race toward the hoop. Dunc flips the ball over his shoulder . . . right into your hands!

You leap, laying the ball on the backboard and sinking the shot.

Miles is furious that you tricked him. When he gets the ball again, he hurries it down the court, pulling up and shooting a three-pointer.

The Viper defenders switch to a full-court press. They're doing all they can to get back into the game. And it's working. You can't seem to get the ball up the court. Their aggressive play infuriates you.

You're frustrated, and as Miles brings the ball up the court, you reach in and swat at the ball.

The ref blows the whistle. "Reaching foul!" he says, pointing at you. The Vipers get the ball on the sideline for an inbound pass.

Turn the page.

Brent, the Viper forward, passes the ball in to Miles. He races up the court.

You crouch low, shuffling your feet and keeping pace with Miles on defense. You're not going to let him get past you.

"Oof!" It feels like you've run into a wall. In fact, the Viper center, Damian Osgood, has set a pick on you. Miles scurries past.

"Switch!" you yell to Dunc, who was defending the center. He should be taking Miles, but he's caught up on the far side of the court. That leaves you to defend both Miles and Damian!

They both move toward the hoop.

To dart over and cover Miles, go to page 23.
To stick with covering the center, turn to page 24.

I have to cover Miles, you think. *He's my responsibility.*

But as you dash over, Damian's arm lashes out and strikes you in the chest. You bend over, both hands on your knees. The ref calls a foul on Damian.

"Come on out!" Coach Willis says, waving you to the sidelines.

You slump into a chair. "Hudson! You're in!" Coach says. Hudson Hart, a lean bench player, hustles onto the court.

"You okay?" Coach asks. You nod.

As you sit, the Vipers go on a scoring streak. You're itching to get back into the game.

That will have to wait until the second half. As the buzzer sounds for halftime, the Tigers hold a slim three-point lead over the Vipers.

Turn to page 38.

"Switch!" you call again, just to be sure Dunc heard you.

He did, and he hurries over to cover Miles as the Viper point guard breaks down the lane.

That leaves you to cover Damian, who's about a foot taller than you. You're outmatched but doing your best.

Miles pulls up before he reaches Dunc and arcs a fadeaway jump shot at the hoop. It misses, clanging off the rim and heading right toward you and Damian!

Damian nabs the ball out of the air. He quickly puts up a shot. You jump up and swat at the ball, accidentally hitting Damian in the arm instead.

Tweep!

The ref calls you for the shooting foul.

"Shooting two!" the ref adds as everyone lines up for the free throws.

Damian goes to the line. He dribbles twice, exhales, and spins the ball. Then he puts up the first free throw.

Swish!

He does the same for the second shot.

The momentum has swung in the Vipers' favor. As the final minutes of the first half tick away, they come roaring back. By the time the buzzer sounds at the half, the Tigers are holding the slimmest of leads.

Turn to page 38.

You've reached the championship game by playing your style of basketball. Calm, cool, and collected. But if you want to break the curse and keep pace with the Vipers, you're going to need to do more than that. You've heard people talk about playing up to your opponent's level. That's what you need to do.

You hurry down the court, trying to catch the Vipers unprepared. As the Tigers scramble to get into position, you push the ball down the lane, dribbling quickly.

Miles is ready for you. He swats the ball from your hand. It careens away, landing in the hands of the Viper center, Damian Osgood.

The Vipers take the ball down the court, quickly scoring again.

"Slow it down!" Coach Willis urges from the bench.

You don't, though. The next time down the court, you quickly dish the ball to Dunc under the hoop. He hooks a shot off the backboard and into the basket.

Turn the page.

The Vipers aren't slowing down. As the first half continues, you find yourself racing from one end of the court to the other.

And Miles doesn't seem to be slowing down. You gasp as you hurry down the court after him. He dribbles to the top of the key before you can reach him. He feeds the ball to Damian, who arcs the ball back out to the Viper small forward. He drains an easy jump shot.

You're winded, and part of you hopes Coach Willis will call a time-out. But he doesn't. He's anxiously pacing the sideline.

The next time the Vipers have the ball, you consider calling a time-out yourself. Or maybe asking a teammate to switch defensive positions with you. You're afraid you won't be able to handle Miles much longer.

To continue playing defense on Miles, go to page 29.

To ask a teammate to switch, turn to page 33.

No, you think. Miles is my responsibility. I've got this.

And so you keep playing defense on Miles. As he brings the ball up the court, you dig down to find more strength. Take a deep breath. Steady yourself.

Miles fakes right, then dribbles between his legs and breaks to the left. You stumble but are able to follow him. He goes to dish the ball, pulling up and clutching the ball in both hands. You drape yourself all over him, not letting him get the pass off.

Miles throws out his elbows, waving them back and forth.

Another Viper races up behind him, and Miles is able to get past your defense, feeding the ball to him.

The Viper player puts up the shot and misses!

Turn the page.

Damian gets the rebound, and Miles slips around you. He's caught you completely off guard. If you weren't so tired, you would have stayed with him.

Damian fakes a shot, then bounces the ball back to Miles. You're trailing him as he slips down the lane toward the hoop.

You've got a bead on the ball, but it may be best to just foul Miles before he shoots.

To go for the ball, go to page 31.
To try to foul Miles, turn to page 43.

Miles dashes down the lane. He's quick, but maybe that's not an advantage. You notice his dribbling is sloppy.

I don't need to foul him, you think. *I'll just go for the ball.* You dart your arm around his left side, being sure not to touch him as you swat at the ball.

You miss! But your action has thrown Miles off his rhythm. He goes up for the layup, but the ball bricks off the bottom of the rim.

Charlie comes down with the rebound. You stumble, falling to one knee as Charlie looks to pass the ball to you. Instead, he brings it up the court.

The Tigers are still playing with the same intensity as the Vipers. As Charlie reaches midcourt, he sees Dunc open under the hoop. He passes the ball hard and fast to the center, who spins and slides a perfectly arced shot off his fingertips.

Turn the page.

The ball drops in.

This change in momentum is enough to propel the Tigers into the lead. When the buzzer sounds at halftime, you're ahead of the Vipers by six points.

Turn to page 38.

You suck in a deep breath, the air stinging your lungs. Miles has run you ragged the whole first quarter. You're afraid he'll take advantage of your tiredness as the game continues.

"Hey, Saddiq," you say, getting the other guard's attention. The Viper he's defending, a kid named Eliot Musgrave, isn't as fast as Miles. Saddiq doesn't look nearly as tired as you. "Can we switch it up?"

Saddiq looks at Miles, then back at you. He nods. "Sure thing," he says, hurrying over to the Viper point guard.

The switch is just what you needed. Defending Eliot is enough to regain your energy, while Saddiq is able to keep Miles to only a single bucket.

Turn the page.

As you jog onto the court for the start of the second quarter, you sidle up to Saddiq. "Switch back?" you ask.

He bumps your fist. "Got it."

You hustle over to Miles. "Miss me?" you ask him as Damian inbounds the pass to Miles. You quickly steal it midair and hurry down the court.

You pull up at the free-throw line and put up a jump shot. It rattles around the rim and falls through.

The end of the first half looms, and the score is close.

"Time-out!" Coach Willis calls. The ref blows the whistle, and you all jog over.

"Huddle up," the coach says. He kneels in the center of the huddle, scribbling on his clipboard. "Here's the play we're going to run."

He draws it out quickly, and you can see the confused looks on the other players' faces. It's a play you've never run.

The whistle sounds again, and you have to hurry back onto the court. Charlie inbounds the ball to you, and you slow down the game.

Coach nods at you to run the play. But then you recall the confused looks in the huddle. Besides, Liu is open in the corner, and he's your best three-point shooter.

To run the coach's confusing play, turn to page 36.
To pass the ball to an open Liu, turn to page 46.

Sure, the play is confusing. But you trust Coach Willis. When he gives you a play to run, you run it. So even though Liu is open in the corner, you stop at the top of the key and call for the play.

The guys run the play surprisingly well! Charlie and Liu cross under the hoop, while Dunc runs up to the line. That clears the area under the hoop, and Saddiq breaks for it. You lob the ball up over Dunc and right into Saddiq's hands. The defenders rush in, leaving Charlie and Liu open in the corner.

Saddiq dishes the ball out to Charlie, who puts up the three-pointer.

"Nothin' but net!" Charlie says as the ball drops in.

You look up at the clock. There's less than a minute left in the half, and Charlie's shot has broken a tie and given you a lead.

Miles hustles the ball up the court, but the Vipers are unable to score.

Bzzzzzttt!

The first half is over, and the Tigers hold a slim lead. If you're going to win, you're going to need a strong second half.

Turn the page.

"All right, guys!" Coach Willis says. "We had some great moments in the first half. A few setbacks here and there, but you've made it this far. I want that same level of intensity in the second half. We do that, and this dumb curse will be a thing of the past."

At the mention of the Edgeview Curse, you see a couple of guys squirm. Charlie adjusts his lucky socks.

You do the same.

Once you're back on the court, however, all that fades away. Or so you think. When Saddiq passes the ball to Charlie and Charlie shoots, the ball misses the hoop entirely.

"Nice air ball," Miles says, snickering as the Vipers get the rebound.

Turn the page.

A minute later, Charlie is fouled while shooting a fadeaway jumper. When he goes to the line, he bricks both free throws.

Something's up, you think as you jog over to him. "Calm down," you tell him. "Just relax, and you'll be fine."

But do you believe your own words? The next time you bring the ball up the court, you notice the Vipers are leaving Charlie wide open. They don't believe he can make a shot.

Do you?

To pass the ball to Charlie, go to page 41.
To find another open Tiger, turn to page 47.

Sure, Charlie has missed a few shots. And he's likely letting his superstition get the better of him. But he's a great player, and the fact that the Vipers are leaving him wide open is ridiculous.

You quickly feed him the ball. His eyes grow wide as the ball comes his way. But then he sees the wide-open three-pointer he has in front of him. He pivots, aims, and puts up the shot.

Swish!

"Yes!" you shout. "Great shot, Charlie!"

Charlie smiles. He bends down and adjusts his lucky socks. Then he points at you and says, "I'm back!"

Turn the page.

Charlie's three is the momentum shift the Tigers need to start the second half. As time ticks on, the game stays in your favor. But that doesn't mean the Vipers aren't giving you a run for your money.

Near the end of the fourth quarter, the Vipers take a one-point lead, their first of the game.

"Time-out!" Coach calls.

The team huddles, and you look out into the crowd. You see Nick, and it makes you think about the curse. When the huddle breaks, you realize you didn't hear the coach's play call.

The inbound pass comes your way. But you have no idea what to do. Liu and Dunc are both open. Seconds tick away.

To pass the ball to Dunc, turn to page 48.
To pass the ball to Liu, turn to page 49.

Miles is on his way to making an easy layup. But you remember Coach Willis telling you at practice earlier in the week that Miles is iffy at the free-throw line. You make a quick decision.

Miles is about to go up for the shot, raising his right arm with the ball. You slide your left arm around his chest to foul him before he can shoot. But he gets the shot off, the ball arcing toward the hoop. Even worse, he stumbles after he shoots. The two of you, tangled together, fall to a heap on the court floor.

From the floor, you watch as the ball rattles around the rim and drops in.

Tweep! The ref blows his whistle and points at you. Miles is going to the free-throw line for an extra shot.

Turn the page.

But something else worries you more. The pain in your arm is intense. You curl your fingers into a fist and cringe.

Coach Willis jogs over. "You OK?" he asks.

You shake your head. You know the curse has gotten the best of you. You'll be riding the bench the rest of the game.

You can only watch as the Vipers score an easy victory.

THE END

To follow another path, turn to page 11.
To learn more about basketball, turn to page 103.

An open Liu is too good to pass up. You quickly dish him the ball, and he puts up the shot.

It bricks off the rim.

Dunc and Damian both go for the rebound and collide. Dunc steps on Damian's ankle, and his own ankle twists sharply.

"Ahh!" Dunc falls to the court.

It's clear Dunc will need to ice it, and he's unlikely to return to the game. Saddiq helps Dunc out. Then you see Coach glaring at you.

"Hudson, you're in," Coach says. You sit on the bench.

"I told you to run the play," Coach Willis says. You're still on the bench when the Vipers pull away to win the championship.

THE END
To follow another path, turn to page 11.
To learn more about basketball, turn to page 103.

Charlie sees you looking his way, but then you spy Dunc with his hand up and feed him the ball instead. Dunc turns and drains the easy shot.

"Nice one!" You bump fists with Dunc as you jog down the court.

The Tigers never let up and soar into the fourth quarter with a commanding lead. It looks like you're going to break the jinx. And when the final buzzer sounds, you celebrate an amazing victory!

But you look over and see Charlie sulking. He didn't score in the second half. When you really think about it, you don't even recall him getting the ball.

Sure, you won. But you did it at the cost of your teammate's pride and confidence. That kind of victory feels pretty hollow.

THE END

To follow another path, turn to page 11.
To learn more about basketball, turn to page 103.

Dunc is elbowing with Damian Osgood, the Viper center. But he's ready for the pass. You rocket the ball down to him with seconds left. Dunc takes it, spins, and puts up the shot.

Clang! He misses! But then . . .

Tweep! "Foul on the Vipers!" the ref shouts, pointing to Damian.

Dunc goes to the line. If he makes both shots, you'll win. When Dunc misses the first shot, you whisper to him, "You got this. Make it and we'll go to OT."

You cross your fingers. But then you hear Dunc whisper, "We're cursed." And sure enough, he misses the second free throw.

You've lost the game.

THE END
To follow another path, turn to page 11.
To learn more about basketball, turn to page 103.

Time is running out. Dunc is in the paint, throwing elbows. And Miles is shadowing you closely. So when you see Liu get open on the right side of the court, you quickly feed him the ball.

He doesn't have a great shot, but there's no time. He puts up a jump shot that arcs through the air.

Nothing but net!

The buzzer sounds, and the Tigers race onto the court to celebrate. Coach Willis bellows, "We've done it! We've broken the Edgeview Curse!"

A first-place trophy will finally find its place in the school's trophy case!

THE END

To follow another path, turn to page 11.
To learn more about basketball, turn to page 103.

CHAPTER 3

SCORING MACHINE

Your jump shot is the best on the team. You and Nick have been practicing it at home all season. So when Coach Willis says you're starting at small forward, you're not surprised. Your shooting skills and speed are perfect for the position.

"All right, guys," Coach Willis says. "Let's go out and win a championship!"

The crowd waiting for you in the gym is electric. It's the biggest crowd you've had all season. Many of them are clearly curious to see if you have what it takes to break the Edgeview Curse.

Dunc lines up against the Viper center, Damian Osgood, for the tip-off. The ref tosses the ball high. Dunc is able to swat it first, sending it in Saddiq's direction.

Turn the page.

Saddiq, at point guard, brings the ball up the court. You line up to his left, break for the hoop, then stop and come back out. He feeds you the ball, and you go for a shot. Your confidence builds as you score the first points of the game.

The Vipers are fast and intense, though. Their point guard, Miles Ortega, is the best player in the league. Saddiq is having a tough time guarding him. The Vipers lead the game for most of the first half.

You need to change that. Fast.

As Saddiq brings the ball up the court, you flash out to the key, setting a pick on Miles and giving Saddiq a chance to drive. You spin, opening up and finding yourself alone at the top of the key. Saddiq sees you and dishes you the ball. But a defender is coming up fast to guard you.

To pass to an open Dunc, go to page 53.
To take the shot yourself, turn to page 55.

Dunc is in the paint, boxing out Damian and getting himself open. You fake a jump shot, sending the Viper defender off his feet. With the defender off-balance, you rocket a bounce pass around him, right into Dunc's hands.

Dunc, still battling with Damian, spins to put up the shot. But Damian juts out an elbow and unintentionally clips Dunc in the chin.

Dunc lets go of the ball and bends over, stunned and hurt.

Tweep!

"Foul on the Vipers!" the ref calls out, pointing to Damian.

Dazed, Dunc goes to the foul line. He misses both free throws.

Turn the page.

Coach Willis pulls Dunc out for the rest of the first half. You can feel the change in momentum without Dunc. The Vipers take full advantage. When the buzzer sounds at the end of the first half, they have a commanding lead.

Dunc steps out onto the court to start the second half. "I'm not going to let that curse stop me," he says, rubbing his chin.

And it seems like he's right. You pull close to the Vipers in the second half.

With seconds left on the clock, Dunc has the ball in the paint. He goes up for the shot, and it bricks off the rim.

It's heading in your direction!

To go after the rebound, turn to page 67.
To see where the ball comes down, turn to page 68.

Dunc is open. A Viper defender is racing to cover you. But your team needs a spark. And you're a step away from being behind the three-point line.

You step back, raising the ball to shoot. But you pump-fake, and the Viper falls for it. He leaps into the air to swat the shot away and sails right past you, leaving you with an open shot.

Nothing but net.

"Nice shot!" Coach Willis shouts from the sidelines. You can barely hear him over the roar of the crowd.

You sense a change in the air. The momentum has shifted in the Tigers' favor.

Turn the page.

The next time down the court, you sink another jumper. Then a third. You're on a roll! The Tigers are back in the game, and it's all thanks to you! You're carrying the team.

As you jog back on defense, though, you see Charlie and Liu whispering to one another. Charlie throws a nasty glance in your direction. They can't possibly be upset about your shooting streak, can they?

After Damian sinks a hook shot for the Vipers, keeping their lead narrow, Saddiq brings the ball to midcourt. Liu is on the left side alongside you. Saddiq passes the ball your way, but it's knocked away by a Viper.

You and Liu both have a shot at grabbing it before it goes out-of-bounds.

To let Liu go after the ball, go to page 57.
To go after the ball, turn to page 69.

You've got a shot at the ball, but so does Liu. Your mind flashes back to the looks your teammates were giving you.

You stop in your tracks. Liu snags the ball cleanly, quickly passing it to Charlie in the corner. Charlie is covered, though, and he passes it to you.

In an effort to gain back your team's respect, you quickly pass the ball over to Saddiq. Saddiq takes the shot.

Swish! He makes it!

By the time the buzzer sounds at the half, the Tigers have clawed their way back into the game.

"Great job, guys!" Coach Willis says in the locker room at halftime. "Remember, teamwork is what's gonna help us win this game. Got it?" The team responds with a loud, "Yes, sir!"

Turn the page.

"This curse everyone's thinking about?" Coach Willis continues. "It means nothing. And if you continue to work together, you'll prove it."

"We can do this, guys!" you blurt out. The team looks your way. Smiles cross their faces. They're starting to believe.

The second half starts strong. Charlie sinks a pair of three-pointers, tugging on his lucky socks after each one. Saddiq leads with confidence. And you show off your jump shot.

Miles and the Vipers are beyond frustrated. The Tigers are almost in the lead.

After a missed shot by Damian, Dunc gets the rebound and passes it to you. You hurry the ball down the court. Charlie is keeping pace with you, but so is Miles. It's a two-on-one fast break!

To fake the pass and take it yourself, turn to page 60.
To pass the fast break off to Charlie, turn to page 70.

You've been dishing the ball off most of the second half and assume that's what Miles thinks you'll do now too. So instead of passing the ball to Charlie, who has a bad angle at the hoop, you fake the pass. Miles bites, stepping back and giving you extra room to drive to the hoop.

You put up the shot and feel Miles swiping you on the wrist. The ball rattles around the rim and falls in.

Tweep!

"Foul!" the ref shouts. "One free throw!"

You have a shot at making it a three-point play!

You toe the free-throw line and take a deep breath. You spin the ball in your hands, then dribble once. Twice. Set. And shoot.

Swish!

With that play, the Tigers have taken
the lead!

You hold on to that lead as the game nears its
end. But then the Vipers land a three-pointer,
followed by a turnover and an easy layup.
Suddenly you're down two points with seconds
to go!

Saddiq brings the ball down the court. He
passes off to you. You can feel the seconds ticking
away. What do you do? Dunc is fighting it out
with Damian in the paint. And you don't have
the best shot.

But there's Saddiq, open at the top of the key,
behind the three-point line.

To pass back to Saddiq, who is open for the three-pointer,
turn to page 62.
To pass the ball to Dunc for a two-pointer, turn to page 72.

You quickly feed Saddiq the ball, and he puts up the shot.

The world moves in slow motion. The ball arcs high. You hold your breath. The ball hits the front of the rim, bounces back, ricochets off the backboard, and drops through the hoop.

BZZZZZZTTT!

Time expires, and Saddiq's three-pointer wins the game!

Tweep!

The ref's whistle stops the celebration short.

"What's going on?" you ask.

The ref points at Saddiq's left foot. His toe is over the three-point line. "On the line," the ref explains. "Sorry, but the shot only counts for two points, not three."

Your heart sinks. There's confusion in the stands as Tigers fans try to figure out what's happening. But then the referee makes it clear by blowing his whistle again and shouting, "Overtime!"

Coach Willis huddles you together. "OK, guys," he says. He has to talk loud to be heard over the crowd. The whole gym must be able to feel that the curse could end today, as they're cheering louder than ever. "Take a deep breath and relax. You're tired, I get that. But now's the time to dig down and find that extra bit of strength."

"Let's go, Tigers!" you shout.

"Tigers . . . ROAR!" the whole team replies.

You take the court, glancing at your teammates. They may sound fired up, but they look exhausted. Fortunately, the Vipers look the same.

Turn the page.

The Vipers get the tip-off, and Miles takes the ball down for an easy score. They may look tired, but they're definitely not playing that way.

Overtime is a battle. The Tigers try to keep pace with the Vipers, but it's hard. Saddiq makes a pass that's stolen, and Dunc has an easy shot blocked by Damian.

Still, Charlie sinks a three-pointer, and you contribute a pair of fadeaway jumpers. You're keeping the game close, but time is running out, and the Tigers are down by two points.

The Vipers get the ball back, and Coach Willis instructs you to foul Damian and send him to the free-throw line. But you've got four fouls, which means you're one foul away from being out of the game.

To let Damian bring the ball up the court, turn to page 66.

To foul Damian, turn to page 74.

You've got one foul left, but you don't want to use it. Still, that's what Coach Willis asked you to do.

However, as Damian gets the ball, it's almost like he can sense the foul coming. Instead, you only pretend like you're going to reach in for the foul.

Your fake works!

Damian accidentally dribbles the ball off his foot. As the ball is about to go out-of-bounds, Charlie scoops it up. He dishes it back to you. You glance at the clock. Seconds left. Dunc is open down in the lane.

To pass the ball to Dunc, turn to page 76.
To take the last-second shot yourself, turn to page 77.

You're down by only a few points. You need the rebound to keep pace with the Vipers. So you leap for the ball as it arcs through the air in your direction.

Miles has the same idea. The two of you collide in midair, but Miles snags the ball. You fall to the court, rolling out-of-bounds. From the floor, you watch Miles pass the ball up to Damian, who breaks for the hoop. The Tigers are shorthanded as you stagger to your feet, and the Vipers easily score, extending their lead. The Tigers can't make any points as the seconds run out on the clock.

The Edgeview Curse strikes again!

THE END

To follow another path, turn to page 11.
To learn more about basketball, turn to page 103.

You're about to leap for the rebound, but hesitate. Miles is also heading for the ball. If you jump now, you'll likely collide with him.

But you're ready. When Miles comes down with the ball, you're there to swat it from his hands.

"I'll take that!" you say as you grab the ball.

You quickly pass to Charlie, who puts up a three-pointer.

Swish!

"Yes!" You bump fists with Charlie. His three turns the tide of the game, and before long, he's drained two more, and the Tigers have pulled ahead.

When the final buzzer sounds, you and your teammates have broken the curse!

THE END
To follow another path, turn to page 11.
To learn more about basketball, turn to page 103.

You've got a great shot at retrieving the ball, and you're not going to let anyone else grab it.

You dive for the ball and accidentally strike Liu! He's swept off his feet, landing hard on the court. He cries out and clutches his right knee.

Oh no, you think. *I've just injured my friend!*

You go to help Liu. He swats your hand away. "Ball hog," he mutters.

It feels like there's a brick in your stomach. You watch as Charlie helps Liu off the court. Coach Willis comes out and helps.

The rest of the Tigers angrily look your way. Your greediness has cost you a player and the respect of the team. It's no surprise when the Tigers lose the game.

THE END

To follow another path, turn to page 11.
To learn more about basketball, turn to page 103.

Charlie is on your left, and he's not good at left-handed layups. But Miles is closer to you than Charlie is. So you swing the ball around your back and pass it perfectly over to Charlie.

Charlie goes for the layup. But he has a bad angle, and the ball strikes the bottom of the rim. It ricochets right into Miles's hands.

Miles laughs. "Nice shot," he says, dishing the ball ahead to midcourt.

The Viper at midcourt races forward. Even this deep into the game, the Vipers are playing fast and aggressive. Your defense isn't ready for it, and Damian is able to get the ball and sink an easy hoop.

"Stupid socks," you hear Charlie mutter behind you. You nod.

The lucky socks aren't the only thing not working. The shift in momentum is affecting your entire team. Air balls. Steals. Easy shots missed.

Nothing is going in your favor.

With all that goes wrong in the second half, the curse feels more real than ever. The Vipers continue to expand their lead, and there's nothing you can do to change that. You lose the game by 10 points.

THE END

To follow another path, turn to page 11.
To learn more about basketball, turn to page 103.

You're down two points. One easy shot ties the game and sends it to overtime. It's an easy decision.

You pass the ball down to Dunc. He pivots, jumps, and banks an easy shot off the backboard.

Tie game! But there are still several seconds left. "Time-out!" the Viper coach yells.

You jog over to the sideline. Coach Willis is chewing his fingernails.

"We left too much time on the clock," he says. "So play safe. No fouls! Do you hear me?"

The team nods.

The Vipers get the inbound pass on their side of the court. They line up, and the Tigers stay close. "Tough D," you remind your teammates.

The Viper making the inbound pass has Damian in his sights. When the play begins, the large center has two players setting picks to get him open. "Watch the big guy!" you shout.

But then the Viper arcs the ball high across the court to a wide-open Miles!

"No!" In the rush to cover Damian, you've forgotten all about Miles. The Viper point guard gets the ball, dribbles forward, and with one second left on the clock, sinks an easy jumper.

It's over. You can only hang your head as the Vipers celebrate on the court.

THE END

To follow another path, turn to page 11.
To learn more about basketball, turn to page 103.

Coach Willis once again shouts, "Foul him!" By sending Damian to the free-throw line, you're taking a gamble that he'll miss one or both of the shots, giving you another chance to tie or win the game.

As Damian gets the ball, and before he can pass the ball off to another player, you reach in and swat at the ball, hitting Damian in the chest as you do.

Tweep!

"Foul!" The ref points at you, and your shoulders slump. "That's five!"

You've officially fouled out of the game. You jog to the bench. Coach Willis slaps you on the back. "I know it's hard," he says, "but you did the right thing." Hudson Hart takes your place.

It's a gamble, having Damian go to the line. And when he sinks the first shot, your stomach drops. He's locked in and focused. There's no way he's going to miss.

Sure enough, Damian makes the second shot. The Tigers fans are quiet.

When Miles steals the ball from Saddiq during the next possession, you lose hope. The Tigers lose in overtime, and you can only watch from the bench.

THE END

To follow another path, turn to page 11.
To learn more about basketball, turn to page 103.

Dunc is fighting it out with Damian in the lane, but finds a way to get open. A simple shot from the tall center is all you need to tie this game and have a chance to break the curse!

You quickly pass the ball down to him, but Damian lashes out an arm and knocks the ball away from Dunc.

Miles scoops up the loose ball.

"Foul him!" Coach Willis bellows.

But Miles is too speedy, and as the clock runs out, he's still flitting around the court with the ball.

The curse strikes again!

THE END
To follow another path, turn to page 11.
To learn more about basketball, turn to page 103.

There are only a few ticks of the clock left. It seems like you can feel each one through your body.

You look down the lane at Dunc. Maybe you can sneak a pass to him. But it's a gamble. Your Viper defender sees your eyes, though, and moves down into the lane, freeing you up for a three-point shot.

00:03 . . . 00:02 . . . 00:01 . . .

You put up the shot.

BZZZZZTT!

The whole gym waits with bated breath. The ball soars through the air.

Swish!

"Yes!" You leap into the air, pumping your fist. You did it! The Tigers have broken the curse!

THE END
To follow another path, turn to page 11.
To learn more about basketball, turn to page 103.

CHAPTER 4

PLAYING THE POST

"Are you ready for the tip-off?" Coach Willis says to you. It sounds like you'll be playing center for the Tigers today. You're cool with that. Center isn't typically your position, but if that's where Coach Willis wants you to play, that's where you'll play.

You step onto the court alongside your teammates. A ref stands at center court with the ball, ready for the tip-off.

The Viper center, Damian Osgood, is taller than you. But you've got a strong vertical and can jump pretty high.

The ref blows the whistle. You leap and swat the ball back to Saddiq, who's playing point guard.

Turn the page.

Saddiq brings the ball up the court. You head down into the paint.

"Lucky break, squirt," Damian mutters, commenting on your size difference. You try to get open, but can already sense he's going to play aggressively. If you're going to break the curse, you're going to have to do the same.

Saddiq passes the ball to Charlie. You pivot, driving your hip into Damian to block him out. Charlie bounces the ball to you.

You spin, driving an elbow into Damian's gut as you go up for the shot. He's draped all over you, and the ref calls him for a foul.

"Hey!" Damian shouts. "He hit me!"

You line up for the free throws. Breathe deeply. Spin the ball in your hands. Shoot.

Swish!

The second shot also goes in, giving the Tigers the first points of the game.

As you jog down the court, you spy Damian glaring at you.

The Viper point guard, Miles Ortega, is the best player you've ever faced. He quickly dribbles down the court, dishing a no-look pass to a scrappy forward named Brent.

Brent sinks a jump shot.

Saddiq hurries the ball up the court. You're playing fast and aggressively, just like the Vipers. He passes to Charlie, who shoots. The ball ricochets off the rim, and you box out Damian, going for the rebound.

Saddiq lunges for it too.

To let Saddiq get the rebound, turn to page 82.
To go after the rebound, turn to page 91.

The way you and Damian have been grappling, it's better if you both don't dive after the ball. If you do, there's a good chance you'll foul him or one of you will get injured.

You pull up and let Saddiq go after the ball. He's got a better chance.

Saddiq doesn't reach the ball in time, though. It bounces out-of-bounds. "Viper ball!" the ref says.

Miles takes the inbound pass, leading his team down to score. The remainder of the first half goes like that. Every time the Tigers feel like they're climbing back into the game, the Vipers go on a scoring run.

When the buzzer sounds at the half, the Vipers have a commanding lead.

Coach Willis paces the locker room. "We're still in this," he says, but without much conviction. "You just have to believe."

You look around. The guys are tired and sweaty. They don't look like believers. Charlie is tugging at his lucky socks. Saddiq is hanging his head. The curse is weighing heavy in the locker room. You can feel it thick in the air.

"All right, let's go, team!" Coach Willis claps loudly. He's trying his best to get everyone hyped. It's not working.

You wonder if maybe you need to shake things up. You consider pulling Coach aside and talking to him about changing positions.

To talk with Coach Willis, turn to page 84.
To keep quiet, turn to page 87.

"Coach?"

Coach Willis turns at the door of the locker room. The other players have already walked out to shoot warm-ups for the second half. "What's up?" Coach asks.

"I'm getting beat down in the paint," you admit. "And I think Dunc would be better at center than me."

Coach Willis thinks a moment, then nods. "I appreciate your honesty," he says. "Why don't we give it a shot?"

Together, you walk out onto the court. The team is already shooting around, warming up. Coach speaks to Dunc, who looks over at you and nods.

When the second half starts, you're now playing shooting guard alongside Saddiq. The change works—Dunc and Damian battle it out under the hoop, but it's clear Dunc is better prepared than you.

After Charlie drains a three-pointer and Liu hits a pair of jump shots, it's clear the second half belongs to the Tigers. You quickly close the gap.

Deep into the fourth quarter, you find yourself down by two points. Saddiq brings the ball down the court. You line up to his right, behind the three-point line.

You break toward the hoop, getting your defender to bite. Then you step back again. You're wide open!

Saddiq quickly feeds you the ball.

To fake the shot, turn to page 86.
To take the shot, turn to page 92.

You pivot, get ready to shoot, and see the Viper defender racing back up to cover you. So instead of shooting, you pump-fake.

The defender bites, leaping up and trying to swat away a shot you don't take. Miles starts toward you. You can take the shot, but your eyes scan the floor, and you see Dunc and Charlie perform a perfect pick-and-roll.

Both of them are open. And there's not much time left on the clock.

To pass the ball to Dunc, turn to page 93.
To pass the ball to Charlie, turn to page 96.

Coach Willis is about to leave the locker room. You open your mouth to call out to him, but stop. Now is not the time to rock the boat. You can handle Damian Osgood. You just have to work harder at it.

This new bit of confidence seems to work. You hold the Viper center to a single shot as the third quarter ticks down. After Liu drops in a pair of jumpers and you make a three-pointer, the Tigers close the gap.

Turn the page.

You're happy the team is working together. But you still can't quite seem to catch up to the Vipers.

Damian hasn't given up his aggressive playing, either. Once, as you get the ball in the paint, he presses against you and says, "What are you gonna do, shrimp? Shoot over me? No way." When you try to put up the shot, Damian swats it away like a bug.

"Told ya," he says mockingly as the Vipers recover the ball.

The next time down the court, you try again. You push and shove and do your best to get open.

Saddiq passes the ball to Charlie, who sees you and bounces you the ball.

"You don't learn, do you?" Damian says.

You grasp the ball tightly, look out, and see Charlie is open.

To take the shot, go to page 89.
To pass the ball back to Charlie, turn to page 100.

Charlie is open, but you want to prove a point and show Damian you're better than he thinks. So instead of passing the ball back out, you throw your elbows up and pivot.

You extend your right arm with the ball, trying to hook the shot around Damian. He swats at the ball, striking you in the arm instead.

Tweep!

"Foul!" the ref calls. "Shooting two."

Your shot missed, so you go to the line for a pair of free throws. You drain the first one, closing the Vipers' lead to one.

"Great shot, bro!" Nick shouts. You hear him over the roar of the crowd.

Nick. The curse. You shake your head, trying to clear thoughts of the curse.

Turn the page.

You can't, though. As you put up the second free throw, you know it's off. It hits the rim and bounces into Brent's hands.

Seconds are left on the clock. And the Vipers are passing the ball skillfully to avoid a foul.

Just then, Miles passes to Brent, who bobbles it. The ball goes out-of-bounds!

"Tigers' ball!" the ref says.

Saddiq hurries down the court. He eyes the clock. Seconds remain. You post up, and Saddiq dishes you the ball. This is it. Brent is coming to double-team you, and Damian has his arm in your back.

But then you see that Liu is open.

To pass the ball to Liu, turn to page 97.
To take the shot, turn to page 98.

That rebound is all yours!

You dive for it. But so does Damian. He catches you off guard, and you both stumble to the floor.

Damian lands solidly on your right arm. Pain shoots from your elbow to your fingertips. You try to straighten your arm, but can't. "Ouch!" you hiss through your gritted teeth.

You stand and walk to the sideline. Coach Willis demands you go to the emergency room to have it examined. "But the game . . . ," you protest.

"You need an X-ray," he insists.

And so you leave the game with your parents. Your X-ray shows your arm isn't broken, but you aren't pleased. Charlie texted you. The Tigers lost.

THE END
To follow another path, turn to page 11.
To learn more about basketball, turn to page 103.

You have an open shot. No way you aren't taking it.

You turn toward the hoop, getting ready to shoot. The defender steps forward, throwing his arm up and forcing you to shoot early.

Swat!

He's able to knock away the three-pointer. The ball falls right into Miles's hands. The Viper point guard smiles smugly at you before dribbling up the court. He finds Damian on a fast break, and the center lays the ball in.

The Vipers have taken advantage of your error and extended their lead. The momentum shifts in their favor, and try as you might, the Tigers can't catch up. It's game over.

THE END

To follow another path, turn to page 11.
To learn more about basketball, turn to page 103.

Tick . . . tick . . . tick . . .

Time is running out. Dunc throws elbows in the paint, but you can see it in his eyes. He wants the ball.

You bounce a pass to him. He snatches the ball, dribbles, and turns. With one hand, he puts up the shot.

Damian swats at the ball, but misses and strikes Dunc's arm instead. The wobbly shot bounces off the backboard and falls in!

Tweep!

The ref points at Damian. "Foul! One free throw, Tigers!"

The game is tied up, and with Dunc's free throw, you'd take the lead for the first time.

Turn the page.

"You got this," you whisper to him as he goes to the line.

Dunc nods.

But his shot is off, striking the backboard and ricocheting off.

It's heading toward you and Damian. You leap up, snatching the ball from the center who dogged you earlier. In one swift motion, you put up a shot and drain it!

The Tigers have the lead, and there's no way you're going to give it up. The team bears down, playing aggressive, smart defense and holding the Vipers from scoring.

When the buzzer sounds, you've done it. You've successfully broken the curse!

THE END

To follow another path, turn to page 11.
To learn more about basketball, turn to page 103.

Charlie is ready for you. You dish the ball over to him. But he's not going to take the shot! Instead, he rockets the ball over to Saddiq, who passes to Liu, who finds Dunc open in the paint.

"Great teamwork!" Coach Willis calls out.

With all the fancy passing, the Vipers are confused. Dunc turns and fires the ball back to you. You're outside the three-point line. A made shot gives you the lead with seconds left.

You put up the shot. Nothing but net.

The crowd goes wild.

The Vipers try to bring the ball up, but there's not enough time. A half-court shot at the buzzer comes up short.

The Tigers have won their first championship!

THE END
To follow another path, turn to page 11.
To learn more about basketball, turn to page 103.

Damian's arm is pressed against your back. He's swatted away earlier shots, and you fear he'll do the same again.

You pass the ball out to Liu. You misjudge the angle, though, and Brent intercepts the pass! He quickly feeds the ball off to Miles, who hustles up the court. He easily slides in a layup.

You glance at the clock. Only a few seconds remain, and you're out of time-outs.

Saddiq inbounds the ball to you.

Three seconds . . . two seconds . . .

You're not even at half-court, but you have to launch a shot. As the buzzer sounds, the ball falls terribly short.

The Vipers win.

THE END

To follow another path, turn to page 11.
To learn more about basketball, turn to page 103.

The game is on the line. Seconds on the clock.

This is your time to shine—your time to show that there is no curse.

Damian's forearm is in your back. He's blocked earlier shots, but maybe you can trick him this time.

You spin, lowering your head and sliding the ball into your left hand. You start to bring the ball up, and Damian's long arms move to the ball.

Quickly, you shift it into your right hand and put up a hook shot that arcs around Damian and toward the hoop.

BZZZZZZTTTT!

Everyone in the crowd holds their breath. It's so quiet you could hear a pin drop. The ball descends toward the hoop. It hits the back of the rim, the front of the rim, bounces to the backboard . . . and rolls through the hoop!

The crowd screams. Coach Willis leaps into the air. Charlie and Dunc rush over and lift you into the air. "You did it!" Charlie shouts over the noise. "You've broken the curse!"

You look out and see your family in the crowd. They're cheering wildly. Nick gives you a thumbs-up.

This is a day you'll remember for the rest of your life.

THE END

To follow another path, turn to page 11.
To learn more about basketball, turn to page 103.

Damian's arm presses into your back. "You really gonna shoot against me again?" he snickers.

You've tried not to let him get into your head, but he has. You think of the last time Damian blocked your shot. The game is on the line now. You don't want that to happen again.

You pivot, throwing up your elbows and acting like you're going to shoot. Then, as Damian puts up his arms, you flip the ball behind your back and pass it to Charlie.

Charlie seems surprised to get the pass. Still, he handles it well. He shoots, but it bounces off the rim.

You and Damian both leap into the air for the rebound. The Viper center's elbow strikes you in the chest, knocking you back. But the ref didn't see it and doesn't call a foul.

Damian gets the ball and passes to Brent, who rockets it ahead to Miles. One jump shot later, their narrow lead is extended.

The Tigers keep trying, but you can't break the opposing team's momentum. As they celebrate their victory, you catch your brother's eye. Maybe next year, he mouths to you.

Maybe.

THE END

To follow another path, turn to page 11.
To learn more about basketball, turn to page 103.

CHAPTER 5

HOOP DREAMS

Basketball is a game almost anyone can play. It doesn't require a lot of equipment, other than a hoop and a ball. Basketball courts are found at parks and schools. Five players per team are on the court at one time. They include a center, who is usually the tallest player on the team and who tips the ball and scores under the net. The team also has two forwards who play offense and two guards playing defense.

Physical education teacher James Naismith invented basketball in 1891. Naismith was in charge of a group of rowdy boys at the YMCA in Springfield, Massachusetts. He needed an indoor activity to keep them occupied. Using a pair of peach crates nailed to a wall and a soccer ball, Naismith explained the "13 Basic Rules" of his new game.

These rules included no shouldering, striking, holding, pushing, or tripping. It wasn't long before Naismith's "basket ball"—initially two words instead of one—was a hit.

By 1893, basketball was being played in YMCA gyms around the country. In 1895, Clara Gregory Baer wrote a book of rules for women, and one year later, the first game of women's basketball was played. New rules were added, as well as changes to the game itself, such as dribbling. In 1894, Naismith asked the A. G. Spalding sports equipment company to design a leather ball just for the sport. Backboards were added in 1906, and the peach crates were exchanged for a circular metal rim and a net.

The sport moved from gyms to colleges around the United States. The first basketball league formed in the late 1800s. The first recorded college game took place in February 1895 in Minneapolis, Minnesota.

In 1936, basketball became an Olympic sport. The 23 national teams made basketball the largest Olympic team sports competition at the time.

In 1946, the United States and Canada founded the Basketball Association of America. There were originally 11 teams in the league. In 1949, the league's name changed to the National Basketball Association (NBA). It now includes 30 teams.

The Women's National Basketball Association (WNBA) formed in 1997. It has 12 teams.

Today, basketball athletes range in age from elementary school students to adults. College basketball is especially popular. Fans look forward to the annual National Collegiate Athletic Association (NCAA) tournament known as March Madness each year.

GLOSSARY

brick (BRIK)—a shot that goes off the rim or backboard and doesn't have a chance to go in the basket

fadeaway jump (FAY-duh-way JUMP)—a jump shot taken while jumping backward, away from the basket but still facing it

fast break (FAST BRAKE)—when a team attempts to move the ball up court and into scoring position as quickly as possible

full-court press (FULL-court PRESS)—a defense where the team pressures the opposing team the entire length of the court

key (KEE)—another name for the free-throw lane; the top of the key is the space where the free throw and three-point arcs meet

motion offense (MOH-shuhn aw-FENSS)—an offense where players move freely to open areas on the court

paint (PAYNT)—the area inside the lane lines from the baseline to the free-throw line

pick (PIK)—when a player sets a stationary block on an opposing player who is defending a teammate; this move is also called a screen

TEST YOUR BASKETBALL KNOWLEDGE

1. Which basketball player scored the most points in the NBA playoffs?

- **A.** George Mikan
- **B.** LeBron James
- **C.** Michael Jordan

2. How many players start each game per team?

- **A.** 4
- **B.** 5
- **C.** 11

3. Which of these teams is not a real NBA team?

- **A.** Miami Heat
- **B.** Anaheim Mighty Ducks
- **C.** Toronto Raptors

4. The player with the ball takes three steps without dribbling. Which violation occurred?

- **A.** carrying
- **B.** traveling
- **C.** overstepping

5. Who was the first NBA player to score 100 points in a single game?

- **A.** Wilt Chamberlain
- **B.** Kareem Abdul-Jabbar
- **C.** Stephen Curry

6. Which NBA team has the most championships?

- **A.** Los Angeles Lakers
- **B.** New York Knicks
- **C.** Boston Celtics

7. What violation occurs when a player uses both hands to bounce the ball?

- **A.** carrying
- **B.** double dribbling
- **C.** double handing

8. Which is not a starting position?

A. power forward

B. center

C. power guard

9. As of 2020, which two WNBA teams are tied for the most championship titles?

A. Los Angeles Sparks and Seattle Storm

B. Detroit Shock and Phoenix Mercury

C. Houston Comets and Minnesota Lynx

10. How many seconds are on a standard NBA shot clock?

A. 10

B. 24

C. 40

DISCUSSION QUESTIONS

>>> Are you superstitious? If so, what are some things you do, in sports or otherwise, that show this?

>>> Imagine you are Nick, the main character's brother. You have lost to the Vipers before. How does it feel to watch your brother play against them?

>>> Discuss a moment in the game where the Tigers are victorious. Now discuss a scenario where they lose. How does each make you feel?

>>> Write about a time in which you played an important game. How was the experience? How did you and your team do?

AUTHOR BIOGRAPHY

Brandon Terrell is the author of numerous books and graphic novels, ranging from sports stories to spooky tales to mind-boggling mysteries. When not hunched over his laptop writing, Brandon enjoys watching movies and television, reading, cooking, and spending time with his wife and two children in Minnesota.

ILLUSTRATOR BIOGRAPHY

Fran Bueno was born and lives in Santiago de Compostela in Spain. Since he was a little kid, he has loved comic books. He was reading *El Jabato* at age eight, a comic book that his father always bought him, and in that exact moment he decided to become an artist. He studied at art school and will always be grateful to his parents for supporting him. His motivation is to do what he does best and enjoys most. He loves traveling with his wife and kids, being with friends, books, music, movies, and TV shows. Just a regular guy? He would agree.

CHECK OUT ALL 4 BOOKS IN THIS SERIES!

YOU CHOOSE

GAME DAY **BASKETBALL**

47 CHOICES
20 ENDINGS

by Brandon Terrell

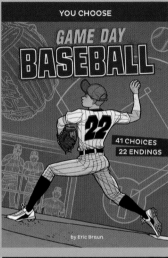

YOU CHOOSE

GAME DAY **BASEBALL**

41 CHOICES
22 ENDINGS

by Eric Braun

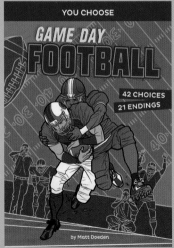

YOU CHOOSE

GAME DAY **FOOTBALL**

42 CHOICES
21 ENDINGS

by Matt Doeden

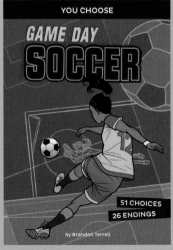

YOU CHOOSE

GAME DAY **SOCCER**

51 CHOICES
26 ENDINGS

by Brandon Terrell